WORRIED

by Charly Haley

Published by The Child's World®
1980 Lookout Drive • Mankato, MN 56003-1705
800-599-READ • www.childsworld.com

Photographs ©: Shutterstock Images, cover, 1, 10, 17, 21, 22 (top right), 22 (bottom right); Waraporn Chokchaiworarat/Shutterstock Images, 5, 6; iStockphoto, 9, 22 (bottom left); Brian A. Jackson/iStockphoto, 13; Jingjits Photography/Shutterstock Images, 14; Andy Dean Photography/Shutterstock Images, 18; Ivan Mikhaylov/iStockphoto, 22 (top left)

Design Elements: Shutterstock Images

ISBN Hardcover: 9781503828131
ISBN Paperback: 9781622434732
LCCN: 2018944236

Printed in the United States of America
PA02395

ABOUT THE AUTHOR

Charly Haley is a writer and children's book editor who lives in Minnesota. Aside from reading and writing, she enjoys music, yoga, and spending time with friends and family.

CONTENTS

Chapter One

EVA IS WORRIED

Today is Eva's first day of swimming lessons. She is worried. Her sister **comforts** her.

Eva wants to cry. She wonders if it will be hard. Her sister says the swimming lessons will be fun. Eva feels better.

Chapter Two

FEELING WORRIED

People feel worried when they think something bad might happen. People also feel worried when something goes wrong.

Sometimes people worry about other people. If your friend gets sick, you might worry about her. You wonder when she will be better.

THINK ABOUT IT

Can you think of a time when you felt worried?

Feeling worried might make you breathe faster. Your heart might beat faster. Your stomach could hurt. You may cry.

If you feel worried, try to **calm** yourself down. Take deep breaths. Think about things that make you happy. Imagine a good **outcome** to what's worrying you.

Chapter Three

DEALING WITH WORRIES

Tell your parents or teachers when you feel worried. They can help you feel better.

It is okay to worry sometimes. Everyone worries. But it is not good to feel worried all the time. If you feel worried a lot, ask parents or teachers for help.

If you see people worrying, be nice to them. You can listen to your friends talk. You can tell your friends something happy.

WHO IS WORRIED?

Can you tell who is worried? Turn to page 24 for the answer.

A

B

C

D

GLOSSARY

calm (KALM) To feel calm is to feel peaceful. You may feel calm when you read a book.

comforts (KUM-ferts) When someone comforts you, she makes you feel better. Eva's sister comforts her before her swimming lessons.

outcome (OUT-kuhm) An outcome is the result of something. You might worry about the outcome of a test.

TO LEARN MORE

Books

Dinmont, Kerry. ***Dan's First Day of School: A Book about Emotions***. Mankato, MN: The Child's World, 2018.

Shepherd, Jodie. ***How Do You Feel?*** New York, NY: Children's Press, 2015.

Spelman, Cornelia Maude. ***When I Feel Worried***. Chicago, IL: Albert Whitman & Company, 2013.

Web Sites

Visit our Web site for links about being worried:
childsworld.com/links

Note to Parents, Teachers, and Librarians: We routinely verify our Web links to make sure they are safe and active sites. So encourage your readers to check them out!

INDEX

Page 22
answer: **C**